D0044949

ORDINARY SINS

Also by Jim Heynen

ORDINARY SINS

After Theophrastus

JIM HEYNEN

ORIGINAL ART BY TOM POHRT

milkweed
editions

© 2014, Text by Jim Heynen
© 2014, Cover and interior art by Tom Pohrt

(800) 520-6455
www.milkweed.org

Published 2014 by Milkweed Editions
Printed in the United States of America
Cover design by Gretchen Achilles/Wavetrap Design
Cover illustration by Tom Pohrt
Author photo by Anne Lennox
14 15 16 17 18   5 4 3 2 1
First Edition

Milkweed Editions, an independent nonprofit publisher, gratefully acknowledges sustaining support from the Bush Foundation; the Jerome Foundation; the Lindquist & Vennum Foundation; the McKnight Foundation; the National Endowment for the Arts; the Target Foundation; and other generous contributions from foundations, corporations, and individuals. Also, this activity is made possible by the voters of Minnesota through a Minnesota State Arts Board Operating Support grant, thanks to a legislative appropriation from the arts and cultural heritage fund, and a grant from the Wells Fargo Foundation Minnesota. For a full listing of Milkweed Editions supporters, please visit *www.milkweed.org*.

Library of Congress Cataloging-in-Publication Data

Heynen, Jim, 1940–
    [Short stories. Selections]
    Ordinary sins : after Theophrastus : stories / Jim Heynen ;
illustrated by Tom Pohrt. — First edition.
        pages ; cm
    ISBN 978-1-57131-090-3 (hardcover : acid-free paper)
    I. Pohrt, Tom. II. Title.
    PS3558.E87A6 2014
    813'.54—dc23
                                    2014018350

Milkweed Editions is committed to ecological stewardship. We strive to align our book production practices with this principle, and to reduce the impact of our operations in the environment. We are a member of the Green Press Initiative, a nonprofit coalition of publishers, manufacturers, and authors working to protect the world's endangered forests and conserve natural resources. *Ordinary Sins* was printed on acid-free 100% postconsumer-waste paper by Edwards Brothers Malloy.

In Memory of Karl Pohrt, purveyor of fine literature

CONTENTS

Part III. *Sad Hour*

AFTER THEOPHRASTUS?

Theophrastus (circa 371 BC to circa 287 BC) may not be the earliest short-short story writer, but he caught my attention in high school where our literature text carried a sampling of his *Characters*. These brief verbal snapshots of people suited my adolescent attention span, and their appeal stuck with me.

Before Theophrastus, there was nothing quite like his character sketches. We can find some precedent in Homer, Plato, and especially Aristotle. But even in Aristotle's analysis of moral virtues and vices, the human qualities remain quite abstract. In Theophrastus we see lively, flesh-and-blood people like "The Toady," who "is the sort of man who says to a person walking with him, 'Are you aware of the admiring looks you are getting?'" or "The Man of Petty Ambition," who "is apt to buy a little ladder for his domestic jackdaw and make a little bronze shield for it to carry when it hops onto the ladder" or my favorite, "The Late Learner," who "is the kind of man who at the age of sixty memorises passages for recitation and while performing at a party forgets the words."

Most of the biographical information available about Theophrastus was written several centuries after his death by Diogenes Laertius in *Lives of the Philosophers*. We do know that he studied with Plato and later began to associate with Aristotle in Athens. After Aristotle's death he became the head of the Lyceum and remained its head until his death at age eighty-five or eighty-six. He inherited Aristotle's books (which were stored underground and damaged) and may have had as many as two thousand students. He was a learned man and prolific writer, whose works covered a wide expanse of human knowledge, both in science and philosophy. His several-volume work, *On the Causes of Plants*, for example, prompted some to label him the "father of botany." I like the fact that his study of plants made him one of Western history's earliest vegetarians, believing, as he did, that animals have feelings like human beings.

Theophrastus's given name was Tyrtamus but Aristotle nicknamed him Theophrastus (god/to phrase)—that is, "divine expression"—to acknowledge his graceful way of speaking. Reportedly, he was a fine and witty lecturer, and some scholars speculate that his character portrayals from fourth-century BC Greek society were models for orators.

Was the audience laughing in response to the recitation of Theophrastus' *Characters*? Blushing? Insulted? Whatever the answers, I never sense real malice in Theophrastus. I hope the same is true in this collection. In fact, I'd like to think that Theophrastus was gently mocking himself in some of his portrayals. I certainly am in many of the stories in *Ordinary Sins*, several of which are thinly disguised self-portraits. You are welcome to find Waldo, if you can.

JIM HEYNEN

Note: There is now a six-hundred-page work devoted to these fourth-century BC short-shorts: *Theophrastus Characters*, edited, commentary, translation and introduction by James Diggle (Cambridge Classical Texts and Commentaries 43, Cambridge: Cambridge University Press, 2004). Diggle suggests that the title, *Characters*, is misleading, and could more accurately be *Behavioral Types* or *Distinctive Marks of Character*. My quotations are from Diggle's book.

PART I

Who Jingled His Change

WHO JINGLED HIS CHANGE

This man jingled the change in his pockets.

It was not as if he were generally a fidgeter. He was not running for political office and afraid that his past would be revealed. It was not as if he were being audited by the IRS. He hadn't just quit smoking. He didn't have a bleeding ulcer or a bad stock portfolio. He had not forgotten to renew his driver's license, or homeowners' insurance, or health insurance, or life insurance, or disability insurance, or car insurance.

Outward appearances said this man had a secure and balanced life. He was ahead in his mortgage payments, just had his teeth cleaned, his lawn fence was in good repair, basement cleaned up, laundry folded, garbage taken out, pets vaccinated, warranties on appliances in order, shingles on his house patched up after the storm, recycling set out on the street the night before the recycling truck would come by, birthdays of his friends and family circled on the calendar, flu shot gotten two weeks before the seasonal outbreak, shoes polished, light bulb in the closet replaced, windshield repaired, oil changed, radiator flushed before winter, crabgrass gotten out of his lawn, tulips planted before the big frost, photographs for the year put safely into an album, workouts at the gym strictly adhered to, thank-you notes sent to the last three dinner hosts, all disagreements with in-laws put to rest, fresh batteries in all the flashlights, toenails clipped and the clippings placed in the wastebasket—and these were just the beginning of what this man had right in his life.

And still he jingled his change, constantly, just jingled and jingled, not even in a comforting rhythm, erratic but constant jingling of change.

THE HOARDER

And for years people thought she was simply a collector!

That was before they started counting: 550 coffee cups, some in cupboards, some on tables, some on bookshelves, and some dangling on hooks. Bathrobes might be a great comfort on a chilly morning, but twenty-three of them? Eighteen ice cream scoops? And two little teddy bears on every step leading upstairs? Collecting knickknacks is not unusual, but a dozen shoeboxes bulging with tiny owls? And what's in all the bigger boxes stacked along the walls? You can't even see out the windows.

By the time it was obvious the hoarder was more than a collector, no one knew what to say. The last person who visited found a narrow path from the front door into the other rooms. Then she stopped allowing visitors because there was no place for them to sit if they did manage to find the path from one room to the next.

The hoarder had enclosed herself with stuff. Teetering stacks and mounting mounds. She was practically smothering herself.

Or was she?

She's sort of like a caterpillar making a cocoon, someone said.

Single-minded in her mission, she went on filling the remaining gaps bit by bit, knitting herself in tighter—eagerly, like one who was preparing for that glorious warm day when the world would burst open around her and she could fly into the unencumbering sky on wings of many colors.

It was a little wiry dog. A yapper. With big bulging eyes. Not a purebred, just a tiny thing she picked up at the pound when it was the size of a rat. It was the only survivor of a litter of eight, and the mother had died at the pound after delivering. It would have been hard to imagine what the ones that didn't survive looked like. The woman chose this leftover. She called it Pee-Wee then, and the name stuck.

She took Pee-Wee home from the pound in a shoebox with tissue paper on the bottom. The dog was so small that she wasn't sure of its sex until Pee-Wee lifted its leg over her two-inch high bronze fireplace cricket.

So you're my little boy, she said, though gender and size were never factors in this woman's affection for Pee-Wee.

When Pee-Wee was full-grown—or at least as big as he was likely to get—he was not only a wiry yapper with bulging eyes, he was a shiverer. He yapped and trembled and trembled and yapped, all the while glaring at strangers with his bulging eyes. Pee-Wee had long toenails that clicked like little icicles and scratched the wood floor. When he ran around yapping in a state of great excitement, he had bladder control problems.

Nothing about Pee-Wee bothered this woman. She held his shaking, wiry, yapping tiny body as if he were the most precious creature on earth. She cradled Pee-Wee on her lap when people visited, constantly stroking his trembling body, and saying, There there, my sweet. There there.

She had pictures of Pee-Wee sitting on her piano. She had an assortment of little sweaters for Pee-Wee hanging by the front door. She had a lavender silk-covered cushion for Pee-Wee to sleep on, though Pee-Wee rarely settled down long enough for a nap.

When people first saw this woman with her dog, some thought she was more than a little strange to love an uncontrollable freak of nature named Pee-Wee. Those who saw them together often felt something else happening. Their eyes moved past the jittery dog and to the calm hands and eyes of the woman. Her affection for the dog moved out and around her like an aura that filled the room. Some felt their own eyes staring, almost bulging, in the direction of the lady, as if they were trying to understand the small creatures that trembled inside themselves.

WHO LOVED COMBUSTION ENGINES

This man loved combustion engines. All kinds. All sizes. He loved the sound of ignition, the firing up—from the calm purr of his large car engine to the fierce whining of his chain saw. He loved them all equally, like children with different but admirable talents: his self-propelled lawn mower, his leaf blower, his Jet Ski, his snowmobile, his speedboat, his motorcycle. He had a combustion engine for his wood splitter. He had a combustion engine for his back-up electrical generator.

This man understood not only *how* but *why* a combustion engine works. He knew which lubricants were best for the tireless throats of the cylinders. He knew the kind of exercise and treatment the knuckles of the pistons needed. He knew how every flexing muscle of the combustion engine needed a regular workout, pumping iron. Use it or lose it, he said, as he fired up one of his combustion engines to fit his mood and the occasion. He was an expert on nutrition and preferred the high-calorie fuels to the wimpy low-octane blends. He knew the delicate ecology of the combustion engine, how everything needed to stay in balance to keep the world moving, to keep *his* world moving. He loved the world of combustion engines the way an eagle loves the open sky. He loved the smell of gasoline as it went in. He loved the smell of the exhaust as it came out. He loved the circulation of the combustion engine, the natural cycle of things.

While others might plan to eat and drink their way through their storage cellars if calamity should strike, for him the key to survival was in the spark and explosion of the combustion engine. Let them eat and drink, he figured. I'll turn to my combustion engines, and I'll be out of here! He kept spare combustion engines sealed in plastic on his cellar shelves. Just in case. Just in case.

THE HELPER

This man always wanted to help, whether he was asked or not. It made sense when someone was stuck in a snowbank or had trouble opening a stuck door. Just the decent thing to do. But there were other times when he surprised people with his smiling face and helping hands. Once he took the lawnmower from the grip of someone who was sweating profusely.

I'm all right, the man protested. I'm in shape and have a strong heart.

Take a break, said our helper, you deserve it.

The helper mowed the lawn and asked for nothing in return. The two parted with a handshake and a mown lawn.

It was when he picked lint off people's sleeves in a department store or stooped to tie a runner's shoelace that people looked at him suspiciously. There was something unthreatening about him, though—mostly his voice and the comfortable way he moved—that made it easy for people to trust him. After he helped a woman scrape ice off her windshield in midwinter, she asked him if he had read that study about how unselfish goodness released endorphins and extended a person's life.

No, he said. When someone needs help, it's like one person is a dusty rug and the other one is a vacuum sweeper.

One day the helper saw a toddler weeping pathetically in a crowded aisle of a grocery store. He swept up the toddler and put her on his shoulders.

Don't cry, little one, he said, I'll help you find your mother.

He held her feet in his hands and turned in circles so that her eyes could be a periscope checking out the sea of heads around them. Look for your mother, he said. Just look around and she'll see you way up there.

The toddler was afraid of heights and screamed loudly and beat the top of the helper's head with her small tear-drenched fists.

The helper felt someone from behind scoop the child from his shoulders. He assumed someone was there to help him in his helping. One officer was taking the child from his shoulders and, just as quickly, another put handcuffs on his wrists.

The strange thing about this story is that you'd think the helper would have learned a lesson. He didn't. He was careful around little children after that, but his need to help was an addiction that no one and nothing could remedy.

WHO LOVED ANIMALS
MORE THAN PEOPLE

They're my little darlings, she said. People can defend themselves; animals can't.

Tell that to a mountain lion, said a friend.

How many mountain lions have you met lately? she asked. I rest my case.

She didn't let her case rest very long. The farther an animal lived from people, the more she protected it. Wild horses ranked high. Polar bears ranked even higher. Narwhals were practically sacred.

Closer to home, she set out bird feeders that squirrels couldn't reach, squirrel feeders that cats couldn't reach, and raccoon feeders that horses couldn't reach. She defended all animals, but she didn't like what she called the "devolution" of some. Like domestic cats.

Cats are an extension of the human psyche, she said. We made them middle class. So now they get cancer and arthritis. They get kidney stones.

Her voice rose as she went on: They're procreating like mosquitoes! Over a hundred million in America! A hundred million! A bored middle-class cat kills a thousand wild little darlings in its

lifetime. Cats are the most species-destructive animals on the planet, and yet we supplement their diet with what they don't kill! You could feed five third-world nations with the money Americans spend on cat food! Not to mention the annual veterinary expenses! More billions!

Her friends waited until she finished. When she got her teeth into a topic she shook it until it lay limp and silent. They didn't tell her how bewildered they were by her diatribe. She had three cats herself, ones she picked up from the pound. Her cats were like feral critters in captivity. She kept them indoors to protect the wild creatures outside, but her cats lurked menacingly around the couch and skulked off like guilty bullies when humans got close. Nobody would say her cats were middle class, but they'd kill if given half a chance.

Her friends still sought her company. In many ways, she was kind and generous. She left big tips for artists and actors posing as waiters and waitresses. She was a devout conservationist. On Thanksgiving, she served soup to the homeless. But whose side would she take if a pit bull attacked them on the street? There was something dangerous about her that her friends couldn't resist. It was as if she were their wild little darling and they her protectors.

THE HARDWARE STORE MAN

He had owned his small hardware store for thirty-three years and lived for the day when someone came in who didn't know the name of the item he needed. Would-be fix-it men gave him his greatest pleasure, after so many years of eking out a measly living selling replacement parts for people's falling-apart lives.

Enter a young man with the kind of glasses that up-and-coming lawyers wore. Or maybe a teacher. A history or English teacher. At worst, a pastor for some liberal church. Whoever he was, he was someone who didn't mind showing up in public wearing earth-toned tweeds and flannel. He wouldn't know a pipe wrench from a deadbolt. He wasn't somebody who lived in the real world of broken-down washing machines and leaky faucets. He headed straight for the plumbing section, exactly where his kind usually went. The hardware store man watched as the customer stood, bewildered, in a world of rubber gaskets, plastic tubes, and metal-threaded pipes of every size and angle.

The hardware store man moved in.

What are you looking for?

I think I can find it.

The customer wiped his brow with his smooth hand. His eyes scanned the shelves like someone speed-reading a foreign document, hoping that one word would resemble his native tongue and that he would be able to pronounce it with confidence.

This was the magic moment for the hardware store man. He looked squarely into the customer's face to force out the greatest embarrassment.

What is it called?

In the eyes of the hardware store man, the customer looked like a child who couldn't find the bathroom. His brow knit as he looked up at the steel rafters, stared into their webby depths as if he were trying to remember some long-lost time when his hands worked with the ordinary drips and spills of life.

Then the customer turned to face the hardware store man. He lifted his chin so that he was looking at the hardware store man through his bifocals.

How the hell do I know what it's called and why the hell should I care? I could give a damn what it's called.

Now the customer moved in more closely to the hardware store man: I suppose you know the names of all these flimsy, poorly made, overpriced pieces of plastic and rubber crap?

Of course I do, said the hardware store man in a sharp, indignant voice.

So what? What has it taught you about the nature of the universe? What has it taught you about good and evil? Why don't you fill your mind with something worth remembering?

The customer grabbed an item from the display. Here's what I need, he said. Oh, I see it is called a flapper ball! Flapper ball! Now there's a brilliant name for you. Took some brains to come up with that name! Flapper ball indeed.

The hardware man was speechless as the customer paid for the flapper ball and walked out.

The hardware man stood behind the cash register. He felt terrible. Anger? Despair? It was just a terrible feeling, but he couldn't think of a name for it.

THE CHAPSTICK GUY

For some reason this man wore so much chapstick on his lips that if he fell on his face he'd leave a skid mark like a slug. Nobody ever commented about it, even though his lips slid around so much when he talked that you'd think he was trying to invent a new language for romance. And he was in a job that put his face in the faces of the public all day long. He sat in a booth on the ground floor of a large office building under a sign that said, INFORMATION? ASK ME.

THE WOULD-BE POLYGAMIST

This woman did not belong to a religion that condoned polygamy, but she felt that God had created her for many men, not just one.

In college—that universal testing ground for good intentions—she explored her capacity to love many men equally at the same time. Not all of her women friends could do it, so she assumed

what she had was a gift. Other young women didn't see her behavior as a gift. Some gave her cruel labels, and others reminded her of those laws that were lying in wait for her when she did decide to marry.

I'm a triple major, she argued. I'm quite capable of making several commitments at once.

She was basically an honest woman, so she was in a constant bind, with more than enough love to spare and no legal framework to allow her to honor her desire to offer boundless and unwavering affection to many deserving men.

She told her best friend about her desires. Her friend said she was deranged and that what she wanted probably wasn't possible.

You can have a harem of women, but a harem of men isn't even in the dictionary.

I am not bound by outworn definitions, argued the would-be polygamist. I can do it. I have the will and energy. I have the steadfastness. I have the love. In sickness and in health, she said. Bring them on.

THE LEPIDOPTERIST

He had an eye for the detailed web in the clearwings and for the colors in the brimstones and sulphurs. He admired the excited movement in the flashers and skippers, and savored the sweet diversity of the fritillaries, the leafwings, and the metalmarks.

Look at that swallowtail! he would shout into the warm, dreamy air.

Ah, and the modesty of the whites, and, oh, such a gentle flutter of that monarch.

To honor the exquisite beauty of butterflies, he used a net with fabric as soft as butterfly wings. To honor their appetites he set out honey scented with rose. He chose a crystalline jar with an airtight lid so that sleep came easily on their final resting place of choloroformed cotton.

He purchasd the finest forceps to return the delicate antennae and legs to the likeness of life. He used the slenderest of stainless steel pins to preserve their beauty, like gems, to his corkboard.

WHO DIDN'T LIKE TO HAVE PEOPLE
WATCH HIM EAT

This man did not like to have people watch him eat. He said that eating was a very intimate act.

You're opening your body and putting all kinds of food into it. Shouldn't such things be private? he argued. Think of it: one second an innocent slice of orange has its orange and juicy presence visibly in the world and the next second it is entering you, disappearing inside your body.

He was so earnest that nobody said, That is rather weird, sir.

He did go to dinner parties and sat at the table with the others. Conversation excited him, but he didn't eat. He used his mouth for talking, nonstop talking, filling the air with his current thoughts on endangered species and the draining of aquifers. One of his favorite topics was the depletion of trace minerals from the earth, though no one could imagine how a trace of minerals ever got into his body.

In time, people became accustomed to him and his ideas, though occasionally someone would taunt him with a question like, Given how you feel about the privacy of what goes into your mouth, how can you stand to go to the dentist?

That's different, he said. That's clinical.

He was a well-built and handsome thirty-three-year-old and did not look underfed. No one knew when he ate. Both men and women found him attractive and often stared at him over dinner as they consumed their food in what he considered their indecent way. As they ate and he talked on and on about an array of topics, they all focused on his lips, which were so full, smooth, and unblemished.

WHO TALKED TO HIS BEES

This beekeeper was always talking. He sounded as if he had as much to say as his bees in apple blossom season. But all he talked about was what he was doing.

Now I'm moving this hive over just a bit. Now I'm checking the angle toward the sun. There. Now I'm walking to the clover field to see what we have this year.

He went on like this all day long, day after day, while the bees went on buzzing about their business as if he didn't exist.

One day a blind pastor was walking through the country hoping to hear a voice from heaven. When he walked past the beekeeper's place, he heard a strange voice over the buzzing of the bees.

The blind pastor stopped and listened more carefully. The sound of the bees was like the golden pillars of heaven in his mind, and the voice of the beekeeper was like the Lord Himself descending from heaven.

I am listening, said the blind pastor. Now he heard the voice of the beekeeper again, saying, I am going to wipe the sweat from my forehead. There.

The blind pastor trembled, fearing that he was a cause for the Lord's perspiring. Falling to his knees, he said, Have I been such a labor to Thee, Lord?

My nose itches, said the beekeeper. I'm going to move my wrist slowly up to it and rub it a bit. There.

Now the blind pastor feared he was an offensive odor to the sensitive nostrils of the Lord.

Does my earthly body offend Thee, Lord?

Just then the beekeeper heard the blind pastor and turned to see who it was. The sight of the blind pastor kneeling along the road with his hands stretched toward the sky was so strange that the beekeeper stopped talking for the first time in many days.

With that, several bees came down on him and stung him, since the beekeeper never wore any netting to protect himself. The beekeeper screamed and swore in pain, then ran to find some mud before the swelling began.

The blind pastor, hearing the ungodly commotion, sprang to his feet, vowing never to wander through the country again. He started walking slowly back toward town where every Sunday he preached two sermons.

The beekeeper resolved to mend his ways also and never to stop talking in the presence of his bees again, no matter how great the distraction.

The bees went on buzzing in their usual way since, for them, this was a very busy time of the year.

THE WORRIER

The worrier was the one who yelled Be careful! when others bounced merrily down the steps to the beach. When she used a Sani-Can, she worried that everything in her pockets would fall into the disgusting recesses of the chemical sewage—or that when she did sit down she would contract avian flu or mad cow disease or the swine flu or herpes or crab lice—or at least be bitten by a lurking brown recluse spider. At home she worried about everyone's schedules and appointments. She worried about leaves filling the gutters and about the nutritional value of food in the refrigerator.

Recently she had come to resent the fact that she was the one who always had to do the worrying. Why couldn't someone else worry about the directions to the airport? Why couldn't someone else worry about money for the toll bridge or proof-of-insurance papers in the glove compartment?

Her biggest worry was that if she didn't do the worrying no one would take up the worrying role and the world would fall to pieces. Chaos. Bedlam. That would teach all the slackers to take up some of the worrying responsibility! In the meantime, she worried about the fact that no one else was signing up for the worrying role.

Worry-wrinkles burrowed deeper and deeper into her brow while the world around her somehow survived in spite of itself. Still, she had to believe the slackers had a heart, that some part of them appreciated what she did. They must have taken comfort in knowing the bills were paid. They must have felt grateful that someone was sniffing for gas leaks near the stove, and checking the carbon monoxide in the bedrooms, and the lead content of the soil in the tomato patch, and the radon level in the basement! When they went to sleep at night, they must have been thanking her in their hearts, knowing that water and rations and candles and two-way radios and gas masks and life vests and fire extinguishers and radiation shields had been stashed away in case an earthquake or tornado or flood or terrorist attack should suddenly be upon them all from god-knows-where. But what about the neighbors? she wondered. What did she really know about them?

THE WONDROUS QUIET LIFE

She was sixty-two and widowed. Church people did not recognize her, but people at the animal shelter did. People at the shopping mall did not recognize her, but people at the library did. In this woman's life, there were more books than traffic lights, more cats than cell phones, more vegetables than credit cards.

In appearance, she looked ordinary in her blue denim jeans and work shirt, her graying hair wrapped tidily at the back of her neck. Her hands had the size and strength of a laborer's, but her smile had a gentle sweetness. She did not startle easily, though she moved through the world with a smooth swiftness, with a confidence that was not aggressive.

She seemed neither lonely nor gregarious. She seemed neither indifferent nor friendly. Still, some curious and good people wondered if she was all right. When they asked her, she said she had what she needed. When they gave her gifts, she accepted but offered more in return than what she had been given.

She had neither answers nor questions for anyone. If she had strong opinions, she didn't offer them. If she had worries, she didn't share them. Those who came near her felt a peacefulness spreading around her. She was like a soft cloud passing overhead.

THE MAN WHO RESEMBLED A PIG

This man had a peculiar resemblance to a pig. A Berkshire, actually, with oddly pointy ears and a squeezed snout. When he spoke, it was like a ventriloquist sending a human voice through the head of a Berkshire pig.

Already in junior high, classmates had taunted him with *oink oink*, so he knew very early what his life would be about. Later, after he had made his way through college and into reclusive work as a laboratory technician, there were still times when he had to appear in public. At first, when strangers stared at him on the street, he'd turn away, but he learned that he looked as much like a Berkshire pig in profile as he did head-on. He practiced a smile that he hoped would distort his features, but this made him look like a cartoon of a happy pig.

Ridicule, rejection—and the face of a pig! Why didn't he lash out at the world? Why didn't he kill somebody, maybe himself?

In spite of his liability, the man was very intelligent, quite brilliant, in fact. Perhaps it was through careful analysis of his situation that he decided his solution lay in assertive goodwill. Perhaps it went deeper than that into the mysterious recesses of whatever it is that makes a man what he is. In any case, he decided that instead of becoming bitter, he would become sweet. That was his goal. He would be sweet—and stylish. He wore a pinstriped suit and a jaunty white hat in public, and he spoke in a gentlemanly fashion. And always with a smile.

The strange combination of his endearing cordiality and pig face fascinated people.

I know, he's weird looking, but what a sweet person!

I thought he'd be shy with that face of his, but look what he gave me!

He's really quite delightful once you get to know him. And such a gentleman.

An extraordinarily attractive woman found him irresistible. He's not like the others, she said. He is the first man who is interested in the part of me that doesn't greet your eye.

Give me a break, said a jealous cynic. The guy's got the face of a pig!

Today the pig-faced man and the beautiful woman are happily married. For reasons they don't disclose, they have decided not to have children of their own, but they have something that makes many ordinary couples jealous.

PART II

What's Candy to an Artist?

WHAT'S CANDY TO AN ARTIST?

The baby decided to cry in public. She was at that blissful stage before words were needed to create a policy. She didn't have words, but she did have a policy. For nearly a year she had taken the matter under nonverbal consideration and had decided, without saying so, that actions spoke louder than the babble she heard around her. She listened to the grown-up babble around her and witnessed how talking was getting no one anywhere.

Crying was a reasonable alternative. She test-marketed her nonverbal deduction in supermarkets and restaurants. Leading indicators pointed in one direction: Cry in public!

Crying in public was bliss. It scrambled people more than pulling thirty books off a bookshelf. It made their faces light up like rain on the sidewalk. Crying in public worked. If a bit of a good thing worked so well, how much better would an abundance of a good thing be? She resolved to work on her policy until she had it right.

Crying at the family reunion photo session one day was nothing compared to the next day at the airport. She wailed and screamed until a whole concourse of men and women and ageless genderless beings recoiled in nonverbal submission. More than submitting, some were transformed. An announcer unearthed a smile, while a janitor swept up his remnants of pity. A lethargic clerk declared early departure. A man in a pinstriped suit inquired about the convenience of buses.

At the airport the baby cried as if the sky were the limit. Cried to the escalators, the baggage carts. She cried to the metal detectors and the boarding ramp tunnels. She cried to the seat belts and tray tables. She cried to the televised instructions for safety. She cried until the desperate flight attendants brought out the toys, the ridiculous non-chokable toys. Toys—and then candy.

Would this candy be all right? they asked the mother.

The mother, already sagging into herself, nodded weakly. The attendants handed the magical red, green, and blue sweets to silence the siren of wailing. But what's candy to an artist? To one who has been transfixed by the glory of being one with her work? Crying in public! The resonant joy of screaming and wailing.

But look: whose face is that submitting above her? Whose eyes are those filling with tears? Whose trembling lip? Is this the final reward of practice, the gift of these deepening wrinkles of fear and regret? For these, above all, the baby is crying in public.

DAYCARE

This mother was so loving, so caring, so adoring, so gentle and considerate—and so encouraging and supportive that her son did not have the slightest idea what evil was. The little boy took such unreserved pleasure in the world that he acquired an expression so sweetly placid that neighboring parents who came into his presence

cowered with guilt. Or resented him: He's like a cake with too much frosting.

Then one day the good mother brought her son to daycare.

For this wonderful smiling little boy, going to daycare was like a sparrow flying into a plate-glass window. During his first hour he did not see the gentle hands offering the colorful jingling toys, he did not see the excited face every time he stacked his blocks more than three bricks high. Instead, he felt the small claw-like fingers jerking the squeezy bug from his grasp to the accompanying snarl of MINE!

Is this the same universe into which the angels of plenty have thus far sustained me on wings of mercy through the land of milk and honey? the little boy wondered. *Or is this but an illusory twinge of misery that I have heretofore known to be nothing but the bell that beckons the abundance back into the abode of my pleasure? Is the cloud of glory I have known, that babbling brook of good fortune, but a passing fantasy before the veil is lifted to reveal the cruel language of take? Oh, woe, ye energies of adversity, is this all? all?* the little boy asked of the crumbling universe around him.

THE GIRL AND THE CHERRY TREE

If you don't stop eating so many cherries, cherries will start growing out of your ears, said the mother.

Eating cherries made the girl happy, and the more cherries she ate, the happier she felt.

Why don't you listen to me? said the mother, but the mother did not scold very loudly.

That afternoon the girl ate every cherry from a whole branch. She went to bed singing and with cherry stains on her lips and hands.

The mother scowled but did not scold her again.

The next morning the girl woke with an itch in her ears. She should have known this was a warning sign, but she just scratched her ears and went outside to start on a new branch of the cherry tree.

The mother saw the girl stuffing her cheeks with cherries. My goodness! she said. What is all this cherry eating going to lead to?

When the sun on her eyes woke her the next morning, the girl had itchy ears again. This time when she scratched her ears she caught a leaf under her fingernails. When she looked in the mirror, she saw small cherry branches growing from her ears!

She quickly got a pitcher of water and poured a little bit of water in each ear. She went outside to find a warm and sunny day. She didn't climb the cherry tree. Instead, she lay in the sun and turned her head from side to side, giving each branch as much sun as the other.

When she went into the house that night, the mother saw the small branches but thought the girl was just playing a joke.

Goodness, goodness, said the mother. Will this never end?

The next morning the girl woke up—not to the sun in her eyes, not to the sound of birds singing, not to the voice of her mother calling, but to the smell of cherry blossoms.

Now when she looked in the mirror she beheld a bright mound of cherry blossoms covering her head. In her closet the girl found a dress that was shaped like a vase. She sat on the windowsill and sniffed the cherry blossoms all day.

When the mother saw her, she said, I knew something like this was going to happen. I just knew it, but you do look quite pretty and you do have a lovely aroma.

In a few days cherries came on where the blossoms had been, and a few days later all the cherries were big and round and ripe. The girl started eating the cherries that were growing right there at her fingertips.

When the mother saw this, she said, Now this has really gone too far. You can't eat all those cherries by yourself. You need to share them with your friends!

The girl agreed, and soon all her friends gathered around to eat cherries with her.

Be careful, said the mother. Don't spill cherry juice all over the rug and furniture. That would really be a problem.

CHILDREN'S PLAY

Out on the playground, the ten-year-olds invented a pretend game in which the boys would be girls and the girls would be boys.

It was the biggest boy's idea.

None of the girls objected but one boy did. Lame, he said. Stupid, he said. I don't want to be a girl.

Majority rules, said the biggest boy, and that put an end to the arguing.

The boy who didn't like the game said, If we have to be girls, let's all pretend we don't like boys. Let's talk like girls and say boys smell like onions and they can't spell *encyclopedia*.

The girls agreed that boys smelled bad and couldn't spell, but they were pretending to be boys so they had to match the boys pretending to be girls by being girls pretending to be boys, so one girl said, Girls can't run as fast as boys, and they look funny when they throw a ball.

The boys agreed that girls couldn't run as fast and looked funny throwing a ball, but they were pretending to be girls so they had to match the girls pretending to be boys by being boys pretending to be girls, so another boy said, Boys are always trying to show off, but they're so clumsy that they fall and then make a big deal of their itty-bitty scratches.

These back-and-forth insults went on until the boys pretending

to be girls had beat themselves up so badly that they didn't have any fight left in them. And the girls pretending to be boys had beat themselves up so badly that they didn't have any fight left in them either.

Looks like we all lost, said one of the boys.

I don't think this is the kind of game that has winners and losers, said a girl.

Maybe not, said the boy. Let's call it a draw and shake on it.

Yes, let's everybody shake on it, said the girl. Just don't give me a limp girly handshake, she said.

I won't, he said, if you don't pinch my hand to show how strong you are.

I won't, said the girl. And she didn't.

THE FAKER

She had the reputation of being a wonderful woman, but her daughter knew that she was a faker. When her mother brought a bouquet of red roses to people who moved in across the street, the daughter knew that her mother wanted the new neighbors to like her more than the other neighbors. When her mother visited grandmother every Thursday, the daughter knew she was just getting grandmother to talk nice about her to the other old hags in the nursing home. When her mother nicey-niced her father—running her fingers through his hair right at the dinner table—what she was actually doing was tricking him into clearing the table and washing the dishes. The faker even had him taking out the garbage and folding the laundry. And his full-time job was just as full time as hers!

The daughter lived with the burden of being the only person who knew what her mother was up to. What good would it do to blow the whistle on her and let the whole world know that her mother was the world's biggest faker? And what if somebody didn't believe her? The daughter's inside knowledge about her mother was overwhelming. It was depressing. It sent the daughter into long periods of brooding silence and occasional outbursts. If her mother was actually as kind and generous as people thought, she would bring gifts to her daughter, not spread them around to a bunch of nobodies.

And if her mother were actually such a good person, she'd show her daughter more respect by giving her some freedom, at least the freedom to choose her own sweaters and movies. And let her skip homework on weekends! And let her have her friends come over after school every school night! But, no, at home her mother the faker was a controlling monster! It was awful knowing what somebody really was and not telling everybody. It was a terrible secret to keep and was probably what gave her acne. And it was so unfair! Why should a twelve-year-old have to live this terrible lie? The only comfort she could find was promising herself that never ever would she be someone like her mother the faker.

THE BOY WHO COULDN'T CONFORM

It started in grade school when he tried to color inside the lines. His crayon had a mind of its own and made a smile into a cat whisker and the leaves of a tree into porcupine quills. When he tried to learn how to play the piano, sounds from the black keys splattered over his C major melodies like spots of ketchup on a tablecloth. Screens popped out of screen doors when he touched them. Vegetables and meat came back to life when he tried to eat them and leapt from his plate to the clean carpet.

He got the reputation of being a little rebel. Somebody who was just trying to be different. The last thing the boy wanted was to be different. The last thing he wanted was people's attention. When his friends put green food coloring in their hair, he didn't. When they pierced their bodies and got tattoos, he didn't. He didn't try anything new or different, but if there had been invisibility cream, he would have spent his entire allowance on it.

You think you can do whatever you want! a grown-up reprimanded.

Whatever, said the boy. He didn't know what he wanted. His mind gave him twenty options a second, like a rainbow on a pinwheel. It was hard to know where his feet would come down or where his hands would wander with so much flying around in his mental universe—and as far as he could tell, he had never chosen his mental universe. From the outside, it was hard for others to see what was going on with him. He sagged a little when he was seated. He sagged a little when he walked. But there was something about him. Everybody could sense it, and they got uneasy in his presence. It was as if he knew something that nobody else knew. Either that, or there was something that everybody else knew that he didn't.

THE CHECKOUT CLERK

She was a teenager and happy to have a weekend job—and the main requirement seemed so easy: Just smile and say Have a nice day to every customer.

On her six-hour, nine-to-three shift at the Five-Items-or-Less line, she served fifty customers an hour. Fifty customers multiplied by six meant three hundred and fifty deliberate smiles and have-a-nice-days.

The phoniness of it all doesn't bother me so much, she told her mother, but after three hundred and fifty smiles and have-a-nice-days, I feel like I've had a facelift.

Be thankful you have a job, said her mother. Most girls your age would give their eyeteeth for such a good job.

Look at what happens to typists who get repetitive stress syndrome, said the girl. That can happen to checkout people too. I might end up needing one set of braces on my wrists and another set on my lips and jaw. My jaw actually aches! The mouth wasn't made for three hundred and fifty smiles and have-a-nice-days in six hours.

We're not spending any more money on braces for you, said the mother. Get used to it. You've got a job. Do you understand that—you've got a job!

Our teenage checkout clerk had read her history books about child labor in the nineteenth century. This is the twenty-first century, she reminded herself, and you can be sure those nineteenth-century child laborers didn't have to smile and say Have a nice day three hundred and fifty times a day.

She decided to rebel with grim silence when she went back to work. But when she got set up, she found that it was too late: the faces of the regular customers beamed as they came to her register.

It's so wonderful to see your smiling face, one said.

I come to this store just to have you brighten my day, said another.

So this was how it was done, the checkout clerk realized as their friendly expectations forced a smile to her face. She saw a life of one little cave-in after another spread out before her. She bit her lip, but she could not stop herself. Now you have a nice day, she said. So good to see you again. You have a nice day, you hear?

THE BOY WITH THE BOOM BOX
AND THE OLD FARMER

This boy did not have headphones, but he did have an old-fashioned boom box that was so big that he pulled it down the street on what looked like one of those luggage dollies people use at the airport. The sound this boy pulled behind him was bigger than the boom box. Pigeons scattered and windows rattled. The boisterous sound covered the noise of a delivery truck rumbling by, bounced and rebounded off the glassy tall buildings across the street. Faces swiveled toward him, first smiling, then contorting in quiet agony. The sound of his boom box filled people's chests, the deep bass notes thrumming on the soundboards of their ribs.

Rather than scorning him for not keeping his joy to himself, a retired farmer, still new to the ways of the city, stood transfixed on the street, waiting for the spell of the boy's boom box to pass. And, waiting, the old farmer faded back into his own childhood when he would sneak up on a hundred pigs feeding at their troughs. He remembered how he would jump into the pen and catch them deep in their consumption. With no warning he would sing at the top of his lungs, The trumpet, the trumpet shall sound! And the dead shall be raised incorruptible!—causing a grand implosion of porcine energy as they plunged over and into each other like clothes trapped in a dryer.

How easily the old farmer came to love this boy and his boom box. What the boy was doing to the city streets was more than he had done to pigs. Better than pig madness, the boy left in his wake a delirium of silent awe. Full of thanks, the old farmer stood with the others as the boy spread his terrific light.

FINDING HER FIRST JOB
AFTER COLLEGE

So this is what it's all about: spend forty thousand dollars of my parents' money and another thirty in student loans, and employers look at me as if I'm a lice-infested waif from the wrong side of the tracks!

I don't like living with my parents, I'm a grown-up. I don't want to live with my roommates, I should be finished with dorm life. I can't

afford good food. I can't afford a safe place to exercise. I can't afford a car to go look for a job—or even to be a pizza-delivery person.

My professors acted as if doing well for them would make a difference. As if their classes in the humanities were a test-drive for real life! Ha! Model student indeed! The only firm offers I've had are temp jobs typing forms for a law firm. That and telemarketing. Telemarketing? Now there's a crash course in the humanities for you. I've tried to get in on a trail-clearing crew on state forest land, but there's a waiting list of eighty. There's always teaching English overseas, but I'm too late to apply for this year. I think I'm a little old for babysitting, and all the waitresses in good places are hanging onto their jobs as if they were tenured appointments. I'm third in line for a job packing remaindered books in a book distribution warehouse. Discards from the Discard? Two nonprofit organizations have offered me nonpaying internships in development that might lead to an entry-level job. In development! That nice word for fund-raising! They want to pay me nothing to learn how to ask rich people for money? It's like asking a death-row inmate to serve on a jury. Exactly like that.

I'm not bitter. I'm too young and smart and energetic to be bitter. All I want to know is what my senior advisor meant when she said I should always be brave enough to challenge the system. System? There's a system? Syllabus, please!

PART III

Sad Hour

SAD HOUR

In this bar, Happy Hour was followed by Sad Hour. It started as the bartender's joking way of clearing people out so he could clean up before the after-dinner crowd came in. When he hung up the Sad Hour sign, drinks jumped from two to nine dollars, the baskets of free peanuts were put away, and the music changed to slow organ preludes.

The first time Sad Hour happened, the Happy Hour customers grumbled and left, but in a few weeks some stayed.

I think this is what I needed, one said, and forked out nine dollars for a beer.

Me too, said another. You get what you pay for.

And so the idea of Sad Hour caught on. When the Sad Hour sign went up, more and more Happy Hour customers started lingering, as if knowing a trend when they saw one. Then there were those who came only for Sad Hour. These were the most sober, always entering by themselves and sitting alone. But all the Sad Hour customers were quiet and polite, laying out their money without complaining and cooperating with the bartender by lifting their feet as he swept up. They sipped their expensive drinks and slowly sank into their clothing as the hour wore on.

For the last fifteen minutes the bartender set the organ music at half speed so that the speakers gave out melodic groans. By now the Sad Hour customers had nearly faded into themselves, looking more like hats and coats draped over counters and tables than they did like people.

At some point even Sad Hour had to end. The bartender waved his arms and shouted, It's time!

There were some sighs of disappointment and occasional pleas for a slow last call, but the bartender turned up the lights and turned on the liveliest new rock-and-roll hits. He lifted his hands over and over, palms up, the way a minister might gesture for a congregation to rise. It's time! he shouted again and opened the front door. Together the Sad Hour customers got up, their bodies slowly refilling their clothes. Calmly, they walked out onto the noisy streets, almost smiling.

THE LOVE ADDICTS

They always found each other, the ones whose hearts had no guidelines. Often they lived within tame and domestic boundaries, but at parties their eyes flitted, looking for gold at the end of a reciprocal smile. In lonely places, their intense light broke through the fog of their surroundings. To each other's eyes, they were bright roses in a dense forest.

It was not malice that drew them to each other, nor a need to conquer or control. It was a pure and mutual hunger. The jealous cynics said their hearts were mere dustbins of appetite. The

righteous purveyors of wisdom said they must be cured, their hollow hearts replenished with wheat bread and broccoli, with brown rice and beans. But they craved pomegranates, ripe peaches and melons. Their hearts were blueberry cream tarts and crème brûlée with Belgian chocolate. Their hearts were a fullness topped with lavish desire.

Look at them now. Don't they act as if they are normal, as if those beaming smiles were merely goodwill? What could be wrong with that lilt of the brow, that innocent grin? And the way they walk—can anyone tell what it tells, their strained casual maneuvers of shoulder and hip? Everything, including their clothing, is snug, a tightening restraint that fuels their urge to break free.

The moment of truth is not like a flower opening to the sun of their embrace. It is lightning and shattering leaves. Uprooted trees, downtrodden grass. They are their own aphrodisiac, smooth and moist and just short of violent. But in the delirium of their readiness, they are not helpless servants of lust. They are not desperate pilgrims on a treacherous frontier. Their marsh of passion does not foreshadow the ashy pyre. This is their verdant kingdom, and they are the king and queen.

THE EULOGIST

This gentleman was such a good eulogist that whenever some-body died, people asked him to speak at the funeral.

I'm not sure, said a grieving widow. I hardly know him and my husband hardly knew him.

You can at least ask. Let him decide.

The eulogist had no trouble with the request. I am so hon-ored, he said. When and where is the funeral?

At the funeral, the priest mispronounced the eulogist's name when he introduced him. The eulogist smiled but did not correct the priest. The eulogist bowed to the cross, though no one knew if he was religious. He paused and studied the audience. He car-ried no notes, but he knew the names of every family member and addressed each one before he began. His expression was compas-sionate, though not sad.

What can be said about this beautiful man? he began, and paused. Mild sobbing rippled gently through the sanctuary.

What can we say of a man who was so truly good, so self-sacrificing, always tending to others' needs?

The sanctuary became a chorus of sad heads nodding in unison.

It is for us, he went on, to celebrate! And then to live! The truths! Of this good man's life!

The sanctuary shimmered with a grieving gladness. The priest crossed himself. Only the widow looked somewhat sour, as if she knew a different truth from what the eulogist was declaring.

We all have our stories, don't we? said the eulogist. We all have our stories of how this man touched us deeply, how his life transformed us—however modestly, because he was a modest man—into someone we might not have become if it were not for him. He made a difference, didn't he? He made a difference for all of us.

Again the sanctuary was an assembly of grateful sighs and nods.

I am humbled, the eulogist continued, I am truly humbled to stand before you in the brilliant shadow of this man's glorious life.

Only the widow was sober-faced and tearless.

Now I, like you, must go on with the work of the world. That is what he would have us do, isn't it? In his spirit then. In his spirit. Thank you.

Amen, said the priest.

Amen! echoed the voices from the sanctuary.

A gentle friend touched the widow's arm after the service. The eulogy was so comforting, she said to the widow. Who is that wonderful man?

To praise the dead is easy, said the widow, but my husband was not a good man. The eulogist is not a good man either. A silver tongue on a sawdust man. His eulogy was vanilla frosting on a bed of nails. My husband was that bed of nails, a life composed of a thousand small but sharp bitternesses. There is no beauty in disguising the ugly truth. There is no comfort in presenting bile as crème de menthe.

I've never heard you talk like this before, said the gentle friend. I didn't even know you *could* talk like this.

I'm practicing my eulogy, said the widow.

For whom?

For the eulogist.

WHO LIVED IN A SEPARATE REALITY

He thought he was like everyone else. He wasn't. He lived in a separate reality.

When he shopped for clothing, he sometimes thought of cutting the antitheft device out of the sleeve of a sweater and walking out with it. In the grocery store, he would occasionally sample a grape to prove to himself what a natural thief he could be. Once he added five dollars to the donation column on his tax return and didn't get caught and felt all right about it. There were times when he blatantly crossed the street against a Don't Walk sign, and he once secretly unfastened his seat belt under his shirt when the airplane was almost up to the gate but before the captain had turned off the seat belt sign. More than once he ignored his dentist's reminder that it had been six months since he last had his teeth cleaned, and then—when he finally got to the dentist—with equal defiance, he lied about how often he flossed. He usually ate too much at Thanksgiving dinner. He twice forgot his mother's birthday until the day after. There are times when he picks his nose while driving his car, and at other times deliberately speeds on the freeway, simply because the car in front of him is going even faster and will probably catch the radar detector before he does. When someone tailgates him for ten miles or so, this man actually fantasizes slamming on the brakes and causing an accident that would be serious enough to put the tailgater in the hospital but not so serious that he wouldn't be able to sue the tailgater for every cent he has.

More than such a gross violent fantasy, this man is capable of actual, though more minor, forms of domestic violence. In just one day he may fail to rinse the bathtub after bathing, and fail to fold his bath towel and hang it up, and leave the toilet seat up, and put his clean underwear away without folding it, and fail to put the cap back on the toothpaste container, and fail to put away the CDs he played the night before.

In spite of everything, while others struggle to maintain civility in thought and word so that the world may continue functioning short of calamity, this man still thinks he is normal and, if he is not challenged, is likely to go on living in the reprehensible world of his separate reality.

THREE WOMEN WERE IN THE CAFÉ

Three women were in the café talking about what they were eating.

Mmm, this sandwich tastes delicious, said one woman. She opened it to show the other women the vegetables that were inside. Would you like a taste?

The second woman reached toward the sprouts and avocado with her fork.

Oh, use your fingers, said the woman with the sandwich.

Then the third woman said to the first two, Would either of you like to taste my oyster stew? It's very buttery.

Love to, said the second woman. And you must try my salad. The house dressing has just the right bite to it.

To make the sharing easier, the women passed their plates around the table.

When they finished eating all their food, each tried to take the check because each claimed to have eaten the most.

My stomach is so full, I should pay, said one.

No you don't, said the second. I eat so fast, I know I had the most.

Not on your life, said the third, tugging at the check. My mouth is twice the size of both of yours put together. Let me have that check.

Before the arguing went any further, each of them started tossing money on the table, and in no time at all there was far too much. But as the first woman dug through her purse, the second said, What a lovely coat.

Oh, yes, said the first. This cotton lining is so soft on the skin. Here, do try it on. What about that velour sweater? she asked the third. Mauve is my favorite color.

Try it on, said the third woman. Are those new boots you have on?

The women started exchanging clothes, helping each other with the buttons and snaps. Some of the articles did not fit the other women very well, but by this time the women had become expert at working out the minor details.

GOOD RIDDANCE

An elderly gentleman decided to take note of everything he knew he'd never do again.

He vacationed at an island where clouds of mosquitoes tormented him day and night. When he returned home, he said, I'll never go there again.

He ate at a restaurant that served tiny pickled octopus. I'll never eat tiny pickled octopus again, he told everyone.

He had always wanted to see the Leaning Tower of Pisa, so he flew to Italy and visited the tower.

Photographs show you just as much, he said later. I'll never go see that thing again.

Then he realized how many things that were near him every day passed into his life and were gone as quickly as they had come. When he left his apartment to throw out a bag of garbage, he knew he'd never see it again, not the garbage or the plastic bag he carried it in. Good riddance, he said.

But then he picked up a pebble from the alley and looked at it curiously. It was the shape of a miniature bird's egg. He held it up to the sun and saw little swirls of lavender and gold. He threw it in among the other pebbles, and it disappeared as totally as a drop of water thrown into a river. The tomatoes in his small patio garden ripened and were gone. The geranium with its short bloom, a falling leaf, the cloud that passed overhead—so many things were his for a moment before he'd never see them again.

For the first time, the quick loss of so many glittering trifles tormented him. He gripped the metal railing on the front steps as he walked up to his apartment. See you later, he said to the railing.

He turned the solid doorknob. See you tomorrow, he said to the door as he closed it.

Same old rug in the hallway. Same stove in the kitchen, same kettle on the burner. Stay right there, he said to the kitchen, I'll be right back.

He walked into his bathroom. Same sink. Same mirror. He turned on the reliable light and studied the person in the mirror. The man he had seen yesterday was no longer there.

THE GOOD HOST

Let me top off your glass, he said to one guest, and while he refilled his guest's glass he refilled his own.

Soon the good host had spread so much goodwill around the dinner table that a good time was being had by all. Everyone talked at once and, even if someone said something unkind, the crossfire of words was so wild and random that cruel remarks were blurred by laughter and cheer.

After dinner, as some people floated off into easy chairs and others served the dessert, the good host told people how wonderful they were.

I would hate to think of this world without you close enough to come for dinner, he said. And you, he said to another, you look better every time I see you.

As most of the guests started to sip their drinks more slowly, the good host drank his more quickly. If someone left the room or looked away, he refueled his glass before any eyes turned toward him.

Then his stories began, and they were longer than the quick bits of talk when the evening began. His long stories started from a sweet center but soon were sprinkled with granules of bitterness. Jokes about his delicate wife started as succulent truffles, but, by the time he finished, the truffles were wrapped in thorns. Other stories had a clear surface but, like some innocuous-looking coffee tables, their sharp edges caught people on their shins.

One thing I'll say for you, you never stop trying, he said to his closest male friend. As the victim recoiled, not knowing if he had been complimented or derided, the good host kept smiling and offered more drinks to those who had sobered into silence. Offered them drinks, then took one himself.

As the evening ended, the good host walked his guests to the door and hugged them before letting them go. As they left, he made promises. I'm going to read that book you recommended, he said. I'm going to call you tomorrow to talk about golf, he said to another.

And then the house was quiet. The good host suggested to his wife that they wait until morning to clean up the dishes. Let's just sit, he said, and poured each of them a cognac. Such a wonderful night, don't you think? I just need to be close to you for a few minutes before we go to bed.

He put his head on her shoulder and watched the shadows hover outside the window.

WHO WANTED TO KNOW
ONE THING WELL

For seventy years he had tried to learn everything. He studied phys-
ics, philosophy, and literature. He was moderately proficient in
Latin, Greek, French, German, Spanish, and even Italian—*non è vero?*
He knew six hundred Chinese characters. He was truly learned, but
the more he knew, the more he saw how little he knew.

One day, sitting in the middle of his books, he admitted that
he didn't know anything well. Not really well. He resolved that
before he died he would know one—just one—thing better than
anyone in the world. That one thing, he decided, would be his
own house.

He started with his tape measure. It took him twelve weeks
to measure his house centimeter by centimeter, room by room,
window by window, door by door. He measured the size of each
shingle, each brick in the chimney, every light fixture and appli-
ance, every book in his library. When he finished, he had forty
pages of data.

Now what? To know his house, he had to know more than the
superficial dimensions of things. His house had to be more than
the sum of its parts.

A deeper knowledge would come through touch. He blind-
folded himself and made a tactile accounting—from the raspy
foundation blocks to the smooth, polished counters. His fingers delighted in the tight-knit fabric of the carpets but were
not grandly excited by the indifferent plastics and Formica. Still,
knowledge was knowledge.

The more he touched, the more he noticed the smells. In the
kitchen his nose told him about potato peels and apple cores, lemon
rinds and spilled milk. His stove emitted olive oil and garlic. If he
paused and concentrated, he could smell cinnamon, cardamom,

coffee. His bedroom smelled like cleaning chemicals and laundry softeners. His office smelled like newspapers and books and, he thought, Scotch tape. Even the piano had an odor, as did every piece of music, especially the old sheet music, which smelled like a small-town museum.

As he sniffed his way toward knowledge, his ears filled with house sounds: not just the familiar starting and stopping of the refrigerator and furnace but the strange sighs and groans as the outside temperatures rose and fell. He listened to the different tunes the wind played on different parts of his house. When he put his ear to the north wall, his lips touched the paint, which made him wonder how many different flavors his house had. Why was the basement salty? he wondered. And what was that spice in the lampshade?

For thirteen months he gathered information, but when he sat down to assess what he had learned, the scars and wrinkles of his house distracted him. Its flaws glowered under his scrutiny. He knew he had to dig deeper. With chisel and scalpel he made his way into the walls to understand the internal organs. Inside the master bedroom he found an old mouse nest. It was round and dark as a blood clot, but it had frayed and softened with age so that air sifted easily through it. As he went on digging, he found the electrical veins had hardened and were threatening to corrode, perhaps to hemorrhage and splatter their dangerous light everywhere—those same vital currents that his house had depended on for decades.

His pursuit of knowledge left his house in shambles. He still had a terrible desire to learn more, but his house just stared at him like a mirror.

THE COUPLE THAT NEVER FOUGHT

The better people got to know them, the more amazing this couple seemed. Neither ever gave the other a harsh glance. Never a snide remark.

It's not as if they never got angry. You could hear them shouting obscenities at the TV when the news was bad or the program was stupid. They'd scold the neighbors if their dogs barked all night. They'd argue politics with guests and shake their fists at rude drivers.

But with each other? Never a frown. Never a Please don't do that or a How often must I ask you! Sometimes the toilet seat was left up, but she never scolded him. Sometimes splatters of her toothpaste were left on the edge of the sink, but he didn't accuse her. Together they balanced the checkbook and paid the bills without demanding an explanation for how the other spent money. They had two children but never argued about how best to discipline them. One day you'd see one taking the garbage out, the next day the other. They were always smiling in each other's presence, so one would assume their congeniality followed them to the bedroom.

How did they do it? They didn't go to church very much and never read self-improvement books. As far as anyone knew, they'd never been to a couples workshop. They didn't meditate. They didn't recite affirmations. They had been married an unruffled twenty years. And no one could count how many marriages were ruined by their example.

COFFEE SHOP CHAIR

The chair absorbed her boredom. When she stood up, the black seat cushion still sagged with her implosive imprint, the four wooden legs lingered in their bent position, and the wooden slats on the backrest kept her dark circles deep in their grain.

Meanwhile, she went outside to be brightened by the makeup of sunlight.

The chair was in trouble.

We all stared at the chair. Just stared at it.

But she? Ignoring the banner of her boredom, she went off into the world oblivious to how much she affected us.

JOB TITLES

The sales associate, the maintenance director, the assistant manager, the executive assistant, and the waitress got together to talk about job titles.

We're all at the bottom, said the sales associate. They just want us to feel good about ourselves, so they stick a fancy word in there. Associate. What does that mean? I haven't been associated with my boss from the day I got there.

Nothing could be worse than to be called an assistant anything. Assistant manager, indeed. Chief go-fer would be more accurate, said the assistant manager.

Hah! said the executive assistant. At least they were honest enough to call me executive assistant instead of assistant executive. When's the last time any of you had to make somebody else's travel and lodging plans? And pack their briefcase!

You think that's bad, said the maintenance director. My real title should be mop boy.

What's your problem? said the waitress. It's so easy, she said. It's so easy. You just gotta go with the flow like I do. If I don't like the way the bigwigs treat me, I just rub their silverware through my armpit and spit in their martinis. Take your titles and just go with the flow. You gotta think. You gotta think ahead about what to do, and then just go with the flow. You hear what I'm saying?

THE DIETER

For a rigorous decade he had been dieting. Like most big fellows, he had tried the Stillman, the Pritikin, the Scarsdale, the Atkins, and the South Beach. He had been to the Diet Center, Weight Watchers, and Overeaters Anonymous. He lost thirty pounds with Nutrisystem, then lost the same thirty pounds a year later with Slimfast. Once he happily lost seventeen pounds on the Drinking Man's Diet. At another time, for three months, he was the only male in a Jenny Craig Christmas season special and lost a half pound for every day in December through the twenty-fourth. His dieting history was the story of many successes.

And with his successes came nutritional expertise. He could give the carbohydrate grams, the protein grams, and the fat grams in any ounce of any food item from Hershey's Kisses to raw rutabaga. He knew the difference between glycogen and glucagon, between monounsaturated and polyunsaturated fats, and could tell you how many calories he could burn in one hour on the step machine, one hour walking, or one hour sleeping. At his size, making love burned 350 calories, give or take a hundred. When it came to dieting, he was a combination of Job and Sisyphus—until one day he thought, This is stupid. I need a different project.

It was so obvious when it occurred to him: instead of pursuing his ideal weight, he would pursue his ideal woman. Books and magazines featuring his ideal woman were everywhere. They were more plentiful than diet books. The more he read, the higher his standards rose. She had to be perfect, and the more he read and the more intense his fantasies became, the ideal woman became a new shimmering mirage. But as his appetite for her kept growing stronger, his appetite for food diminished.

For two years, as his weight steadily dropped and his fantasies of his ideal mate flourished, one day, there she was—his Eve, his

Beatrice, his Sophia Loren! Those legs! That face! That hair! And the eyes that said she was mentally brilliant, and that movement of her thigh that said she was a dancer, and that swirl of her wrist that said she was an artist, and that notebook in her hand that said she was a poet!

He wasted no time courting her, and soon asked her, quite confidently, Will you marry me?

Certainly not, said his ideal woman. Look at you: you're nothing but skin and bones. I hate men who have emaciated themselves with a lifetime of bad choices!

THE ESCAPEE

For almost a year they watched him work out on the track every morning, though he'd reverse his direction in the middle of a lap, so no one knew for sure how far he could run. Sometimes he sprinted and then stopped, panting loudly, as if air were freedom and he never got enough.

It is like cutting your wrist, if you want to call that freedom, he once told them.

In the morning he ran toward the dawn and in the evening toward the sunset, and they did not know what to think of that. All they had was the minimum security of themselves, while he had other purposes. Call it rehabilitation. He had only six months left and a great body. They were still spitting on the sidewalks when the guards were not looking and at best could do this without moving their chins.

Then of course he did it and was only two laps gone when the whistles blew. Now they were the ones who breathed deep and tried to blow him over the mountain without moving their chins.

The first ten miles are easy, he told them later. Then you don't have any skin and your whole body is an ear and the cold wind screams pain and the dust screams pain. You're raw liver to the dogs and anywhere is the wrong turn.

They asked him if he thought of that before he ran and he said, Yes.

The warden would not let him run after that and he started spitting with the rest of them. He was quick even at this and filled them all with resolve and goodwill. There was no way he could have known how much they needed him.

THE GRIN REAPER

When others chuckled, he sneered. If someone laughed at a joke, he stared at them as if they'd passed gas in an elevator. If there were a smile anywhere in a room, he'd go after it with a scythe of bitterness, a sharp haughty look that screamed, Stupid! To say he didn't have a sense of humor was like saying a snake didn't have long legs. When he left a room, you felt that kind of peace that comes when you stop beating yourself on the head with a hammer.

Talk about a wet blanket!
This guy doesn't have an ounce of joy in him!
How can anybody be such a total downer?
How can anyone be so one-dimensional?
No one could explain him, but it was easy to give him a name.

BE CAREFUL WHAT YOU WISH FOR

The way they remembered the story, it went like this: Many years ago one farmer stood in the way of everybody out there getting electricity. Before electricity could come, this farmer needed to cut down his tall evergreen trees where the power lines could go. He refused to cut down his evergreen trees, so it was a stand-off between him and his trees and everybody else.

The boys knew this farmer was a bad man. What kind of person would keep everybody from getting electricity just for his stupid old evergreen trees?

Finally, all the neighbors went over to this farmer's place with saws in their hands.

If you want to shoot us to save your trees, then shoot us all, said one of the neighbors. Life isn't worth living without electricity.

That's the day the boys learned that this farmer wasn't all bad. He let his neighbors cut down his evergreen trees so the power lines could go up.

Be careful what you wish for, said the farmer who didn't have any evergreen trees anymore. The boys were there when he said those words, and they did wonder if he was still as bad as they once thought he was.

It wasn't long before the power lines went up and everybody had their farms wired for the big day when electricity would come like an angel from above and give them all light.

A big switch was going to be thrown somewhere out there in the darkness, and, just like that, all the new and unused light bulbs would come to life. The letter said that it would happen at five o'clock one night. Have all the switches turned off, the letter warned, and then turn them on one at a time so that the wires get used to all that electric power coming through them.

The night of the big switch, the boys sat around the kitchen table with the grown-ups. Then they saw it happen: a light at a neighbor's house where there had never been a light before. Then lights started popping up all over the place. The horizon looked as if it was covered with fireflies.

The oldest boy got to flick the switch in the kitchen. The fluorescent light above the kitchen table stuttered a little—and then it came to life. First a trickle, then a splash, then an avalanche of light. Bright light. Light brighter than any kerosene lamp or flashlight. Light as bright as high noon on the Fourth of July.

Everyone around the kitchen table looked at each other: every freckle on their faces, every smudge on their collars, every speck of dirt on their hands screamed out in this new and bright light. They looked around the room: was this their kitchen? The ceiling where the old kerosene lamp had hung showed a dark and ugly shadow that the smoke must have left. The white cupboards looked gray. The wallpaper was stained with who knows what!

The boys felt ashamed to be in such a dirty place, but it was a grown-up who said, Look at this place! We have some work to do!

They knew what was coming next. Instead of playing Chinese checkers after supper the way they did in the old days, they were busy washing walls. With all the bright light showing them what they were doing, they didn't have to be told that they missed a spot.

IT COULD HAVE HAPPENED TO ANYONE

A farmer yelled for his boys to hurry. Somebody had slid off the road and was stuck in a snowbank.

Here! You take this shovel and you take this one, he yelled. Get in the back of the pickup.

In a minute they moved down the road and stayed safely in the tracks that other vehicles had made in the snow. Down the road, the rear end of a blue four-door stuck up out of the ditch with its wheels spinning in thin air. You could see where the front wheels had zigged out of the tracks before the rear end slid around and the whole car nosedived into the ditch.

The boys recognized the driver. It was the science teacher. He didn't have any gloves on. He stepped out of his car when the pickup stopped. He didn't have a warm cap or warm boots either! He looked like he should have stayed in the science lab. First one boy started to snicker, and then another. When their snickering made them bump their shovels against the back window of the pickup, the grown-ups gave them that stare. The boys put their warm gloves over their mouths.

Pickups and cars full of farmers and farm boys were heading toward them from both directions. Everybody had brought shovels. Everybody wore boots and gloves and warm caps—and they all tried to get at the teacher's car first. The boys saw what was happening and put their grins away. They got into it, shoveling faster than anyone else. But there were so many boys and men there—some shoveling and some pushing—that it was hard to tell just who should have gotten credit for the way the stuck car came out of the ditch like a sorry old tooth that knew it was time to let itself go. The car eased out and sat back on the middle of the road with its grill stuffed with snow.

Everyone stood on the road and looked at the prized car. One man dug the snow out of the grill. Another kicked packed snow from under the fenders.

How can I thank all of you? asked the teacher. Let me give you some money.

Don't even think of it, said one of the grown-ups. It could have happened to anybody.

Everybody got their cars and pickups turned around without sliding into the ditch.

The boys took their place in the pickup and started snickering again. They looked back at the big hole that the teacher's car had left in the ditch. It looked like a science project that didn't work out too well, but it was an impressive hole. For a while, people who drove by would say, What on earth happened here?

But then spring would come and melt away all the evidence. Right now, though, everybody looked happy. Everybody looked full of thanks.

THE SANDBOX

Strangers thought the sandbox in the backyard meant that a child lived in the house nearby. In fact, a retired army general lived in the house nearby, and he didn't have any children. He was through with war. He had come back, bought a house, and lived alone. The sandbox was his sandbox and his only.

A security light in the backyard turned on when anything moved back there, so at night he had to loosen the light before he could play in his sandbox unnoticed. When he went out in the dark, he first sifted through the sand with a cat-box scoop. He didn't have a cat, but his neighbors did. A small yellow dump truck waited for cat droppings. The general drove it stealthily away and emptied it into the flowerbed. Cleaning the sandbox was a warm-up for serious play.

He sat bare-legged on the sand and made different forms, sometimes breasts and hips but usually sandcastles and forts. Being noticed on a night mission could spoil everything, so he played for a half hour but no longer. He avoided the sandbox on moonlit nights when people might see him. The darkest nights were his favorites. In pitch blackness all he had was the feel of the sand, the liquid sound of it flowing through his fingers and never fighting back. He liked the way it found new forms or followed the form of whatever pressed into it.

To cap off the evening, he rolled in the sand, letting it sooth his flesh and cling to him. He bathed in his sand, but when he got up, some of the sand followed him into the house and sprinkled itself over his rugs and furniture. Cleaning up the wayward sand was his daytime work. It didn't take that long, and usually there was only a cupful that he had to sweep up. When darkness returned, he carefully carried the cup of sand back to his sandbox where it belonged.

KEEPING ONE'S SECRET

This man's secret was that he urinated wherever he pleased. It's not as if he was raised in a country where every street-side bush was like a fire hydrant to a beagle. It is true that he was raised on a farm where he learned to imitate the animals in their indiscriminate fertilizing of every spot where they stood—but that was years ago. Today he was an SUV-driving suburbanite who wore Ralph Lauren shirts to work.

The man who urinated wherever he pleased believed everyone had a secret and that his secret was less harmful than most. Instead of hiding a pint of whiskey in his desk, he urinated behind his open car door in a mini-mall parking lot. Rather than slipping off to a casino to waste money, he urinated in the corner of his garage. What's your secret? he wondered when he met a tight-lipped banker for a business loan. Do you look at porn sites on your office computer? Do you cheat on your taxes? And the flight attendant who smiled coyly as she handed out peanuts and pretzels, did she have a different lover at every overnight stop?

The urinator had not had the flu or a cold for ten years, not since he started urinating wherever he pleased. He didn't make a connection. He was not superstitious about his secret. All he knew is that the good life accompanied urinating wherever he pleased. On starry nights, he looked up smiling while he urinated from his upstairs bedroom—in an arc that avoided staining the house siding. Over the years he became so skilled in his ventures that he was never caught. When he seemed to be kneeling to pull weeds in his garden, would anyone wonder why the marigolds were sparkling when he walked away? When he stepped off the path in the city park and returned staring up like a bird-watcher, would anyone suspect that his look of contentment came from anything but spotting an Oregon junco?

Everyone had a secret, but most didn't know how to protect it. They were clumsy or reckless, like shoplifters who didn't notice the security cameras or who didn't know how not to look like a shoplifter. Other men who would like to urinate wherever they pleased made stupid mistakes, like standing with feet apart, with one hand in front and one hand on the hip. Keeping one's secret was not for fools. It required imagination and practice. Keeping one's secret was an art, or at least a highly developed craft.

THE POOR RICH YOUNG MAN

When this young man confronted his wealthy parents about their drinking, they disowned him. For the first time in his life, he was poor. Out on the street.

My parents disowned me and I am impoverished, he announced. I have nowhere to sleep, nothing to eat, no money to buy clothing. I don't even have a car.

The poor rich young man didn't have poor friends, so he didn't have anyone to ask how to be poor. How did one get food stamps? And how did one get a job as a dishwasher or a janitor? How did one act unemployed when the only people he had ever known were the ones who did the employing?

The poor rich young man talked to the friends he did have. Do you know about the bus schedule? he asked. Will I be safe riding one downtown to look for a job?

Don't be silly, said his friend. You can use my car. And we have a spare room at our house that you may use whenever you need it.

News of the poor rich young man's dire situation became the topic of conversation at many cocktail parties.

Wasn't that brave of him to challenge his parents about their drinking? They really were having a problem with it.

I simply adore him for that, said another. His heart is so good. He meant so well for his parents.

The poor rich young man soon had more dinner invitations than he could accept. Everyone's spare room was open to him, as were their refrigerators and spare cars.

Here, take the keys to the Chevy. Here, take these house keys. You can come in our back door any time you need a place—the security alarm code is on this card. And here's a key to the tennis court.

One woman gave the poor rich young man spending money

for house-sitting her cats, another for walking her dog through the park. There were canaries to feed and aquariums to check. There were suits and trousers on their way to the Goodwill that could just as well be given to the young man. Everyone wanted a piece of his welfare. Everyone gave him a key to something.

The poor rich young man learned to live with his misfortune. The ring of keys that dangled from his belt grew so large that poor people on the street nodded in recognition of one of their own.

How many floors must he be sweeping to need so many keys? How many latrines must he be cleaning every day?

Poor people smiled at the young man as if he were a brother, as did the rich, thus giving the poor rich young man the best of both worlds as he made his way through this difficult time in his life.

MAN TYING HIS SHOES

It was not about the shoes so much as the shoelaces. If they were soap, he would have been lathering his hands with them. If they were water, his hands would have been surfing them. He was cleaning their floppy ears! He was orchestrating the shoelaces! The shoes were quite handsome, black wingtips with a real luster, but they were not major players in the drama. It was the shoelaces that excited him and must have satisfied something that others would not understand.

The abrupt quickness of his stooping suggested that he stooped to tie his shoes often. Did his mother not teach him to tie a shoe properly the first time?

Others on the sidewalk swerved around the bulging smile of his buttocks.

His efforts produced two impressive loops that hung down over his shoe like the floppy ears of a beagle.

When he started walking again, his face showed he was not happy with his freshly tied shoe. It may have been too tight, or he might have sensed that it was too loose and would again be two unbowed strands after a few steps. He walked over to a bench near the bus stop, sat down, and retied the same shoe.

This had to be about something more than shoestrings. He must have been trying to solve an invisible problem, perhaps mending a relationship that was unraveling.

He gritted his teeth as he looped and pulled the shoestrings, then gave both loops a final tug for good measure.

The man was in his fifties and should have worked through his problems by now—or at least found a more conventional means of dealing with them, but he was not hurting anyone, and who was to say how a man should confront the anguishes of his life?

He stood up and was off again with his freshly tied shoe, but he was looking down. Something was wrong, but now it was the other foot. He stooped to tie the other shoe, and he grappled especially hard to get it right. Admirably, the man had chosen today to confront all of his problems at once.

THE ARTS ADMINISTRATOR

He had been an artist in his own right. Running programs and dispensing funds was now his way of making a modest living while staying close to what had always been dear to him.

Other artists loved him the way artists love people who have their hands on the purse strings. They told him how good it was to work with somebody who understood an artist's problems.

Most people just don't know what it's like to deal with greedy gallery owners. Most people have no idea how hard it is to make a living writing unpopular literature. You have a heart, man, you really do.

The arts administrator worked hard at convincing legislators and philanthropists to donate money to the funds he managed. He practiced sales pitches on his friends who were not artists. He noted how business people dressed. He learned to impress them by appearing to be impressed by them.

Among artists he dressed more casually, though he tried to emulate some of the mannerisms of those who provided him with the funds he dispersed. Sometimes the funders felt like his parents and the artists like his children. The funders needed praise; the artists needed nurturing. Flipping from praise to nurturing became an art in itself, and he became a master at it.

At night he went home to his stylish apartment. For half an hour he played the piano to relax. Then he took out his notebook, sat at his small desk overlooking the courtyard below, and wrote a few lines of poetry. After cocktails with a few friends, he went to his painting closet and worked on his unfinished watercolors. Then he prepared a light gourmet dinner, sat down at the table alone, and between bites, wrote a few notes in his journal. Sometimes before going to bed he stood in front of the mirror with one of his own paintings, held it up toward the mirror, and imagined himself to be a curious and objective observer.

THE BOOK REVIEWER

When the book reviewer finally wrote her own book, she imagined what other book reviewers would say.

Her book was a strange and quirky collection of short prose pieces that she hoped reviewers would label "flash fiction," though she knew some might call them prose poems, which would be all right with her. If anyone labeled them "snippets" or "vignettes," she would throw an epic tantrum.

A rainbow of earthly delights was what she hoped *Publisher's Weekly* would say.

But what if *Kirkus* said, If no one wished Milton's *Paradise Lost* to be longer, no one will wish these anorexic snippets to be shorter?

What if *The New York Times Book Review* wrote, If the author took any pains to write these weightless vignettes, they certainly were not labor pains?

Would *Library Journal* say, Perhaps readers are witnessing the invention of a new literary form: it should be called *Farts in the Wind*?

Still, she could see a respectable academic journal declaring, This collection is a banquet of delectable hors d'oeuvres, each with its own flavor so distinct that it needs no garnish. Something for every palate!

There simply was no way of knowing what reviewers would say. That was the torment. What if one of them was someone whose work she had reviewed harshly? But, no, she had never been gratuitously harsh, only painstakingly honest. At any rate, it was all a matter of taste, anyhow.

I don't really care what they say about me, she finally consoled herself, so long as they're talking about me.

JOHN DOE

This man wanted to be anonymous. He wanted to be as incon-
spicuous as a flyspeck on a black car, but the world conspired
against him. One day he received twenty e-mail advertisements,
six telemarketing calls, and a piece of junk mail from an insurance company that began with the words WE LOVE YOU! The
same day, when he bought a new pair of walking shoes with cash,
the sales clerk asked, Could I have your zip code, please?

This is driving me crazy! he shouted. I do not want to be
identified by name, by address, by telephone number, by Social

Security number, or serial number. I do not want to be known by zip code, by area code, by color code, or by secret code! Enough is enough!

He started erasing himself by changing his legal name to John Doe.

A person to whom he wrote a check was the first to talk: The first odd thing about him is his name, but then just watch him. He's like a deer foraging in a forest; every few seconds he lifts his head and looks quickly in both directions.

Word of John Doe's pursuit of anonymity spread like a flu virus quietly and inconspicuously around the town. It wasn't long before a stranger on the street walked up to him and said, You're John Doe, aren't you?

It was time to mutate once more: he researched the most common names on earth and changed his name to Muhammad Smith.

It evidently was a curious combination and soon, someone pointed at him and said his name as if it were a delightful curiosity that everyone should enjoy.

Anonymity will have to start at home, he finally realized. If I stay in my house, I will become invisible to the world. But what to do with himself alone in his house? The answer was obvious once he picked up his pen and started writing. Of course! Writing! Why hadn't he thought of this before?

Anonymously, Muhammad Smith wrote and wrote poems and short stories, wrote and wrote until he became curious about what others might think of his writing. He sent off samples. Editors loved his short stories. Editors loved his poetry. He published in magazines and newspapers all over the country. Hundreds of publications that he kept in boxes around his house. To his amazement and deep satisfaction, within three years, no one recognized his name or knew who he was.

ACKNOWLEDGMENTS

Some of these stories originally appeared in the following publications:

Clover: "Children's Play" and "The Checkout Clerk"
Fifth Wednesday: "Who Loved Animals More Than People" (as "Little Darlings")
Georgia Review: "Sad Hour," "What's Candy to an Artist?" "Good Riddance," "The Good Host"
Great River Review: "Who Loved Combustion Engines," "Be Careful What You Wish For," "Who Jingled His Change" (as "Spare Change"), "The Hoarder"
Jeopardy: "Three Women Were in the Café"
Opus 45: "The Wondrous Quiet Life"
Shenandoah: "The Hardware Store Man," "The Poor Rich Young Man" (both in different form)
Sleet: "The Love Addicts," "Man Tying His Shoes," "Daycare"
The Southeast Review (formerly Sundog): "The Escapee" (in different form)
Water-Stone: "The Boy Who Couldn't Conform"
Wigleaf: "The Boy with the Boom Box and the Old Farmer"
Zero: "Who Talked to His Bees"

JIM HEYNEN was born in a farmhouse near Sioux Center, Iowa; attended a one-room schoolhouse; graduated from Hull Western Christian High in Hull, Iowa; and attended Dordt College in Sioux Center before transferring to Calvin College in Grand Rapids, Michigan, where he graduated at age twenty with majors in English education and speech/drama. He taught at Hull Western Christian before four years of graduate work at the University of Iowa, concentrating in English Renaissance Literature. He taught three years at the University of Michigan–Flint and one year at Calvin College before moving to Eugene, Oregon, and earning his MFA in creative writing at the University of Oregon. After several years in Artists in the Schools programs, arts administration at Centrum in Port Townsend, Washington, and residencies at the University of Alaska and University of Idaho, he taught in the Northwest Writing Institute at Lewis and Clark College in Portland, Oregon. In 1992, he moved with his wife Sarah T. Williams to St. Paul, Minnesota, served as writer-in-residence at St. Olaf College for fifteen years, and is currently writing full time and teaching in the Rainier Writing Workshop, a low-residency MFA program at Pacific Lutheran University in Tacoma, Washington.

Interior design by Connie Kuhnz. Typeset in Dante by
Bookmobile Design and Digital Publisher Services.